Do You See
What I See...

This book was designed, produced, and published by Landauer Books
A division of Landauer Corporation
12251 Maffitt Road, Cumming, Iowa 50061

President: Jeramy Lanigan Landauer
Vice President: Becky Johnston
Managing Editor: Marlene Hemberger Heuertz
Art Director: Laurel Albright
Graphics Technician: Stewart Cott

ISBN: 1-890621-08-0

This book is printed on acid-free paper.

Printed in China

10 9 8 7 6 5

# Do You See What I See…

*Illustrated by Sandi Gore Evans*
*Story by Sandi Gore Evans and Amanda Evans*

Lullabye...and Goodnight...

Once upon a moonlit night,
there was a small woods
where the snow glistened bright,
and the trees sang softly:
"hush-a-bye,  hush-a-bye."

The animals and birds
were snuggled up tight—
the little ones knew
it was time for night-night.
But on the forest floor
danced a bright twinkling light.

...Close your eyes now and sleep tight...

The Rabbit family was
asleep in soft needles of pine,
but little Bun-Bun,
entranced by the sight,
could not shut her eyes.
She slipped out of the nest
and hopped into the night.

After hopping just
a short while, Bun-Bun came
upon her friend,
Hooty Owl.
He was always up past
Bun-Bun's bedtime,
and sometimes
wore a serious scowl.

"I'm going on an adventure", said Bun-Bun,
"to follow the light. Would you like
to go, too, Mr. Hooty?"
"Whooooo me?,"
snooty Hooty replied.
"I am much tooooo
busy filling up my pantry
to join yoooou!"

DAY SLEEPER

Just then there was a
flutter from the branch above.
It was Happy the red bird—
the only bird in the
forest without a song.
Even though Happy couldn't
sing, he was still always happy and
delighted to come along.

"I'd be happy to join you,"
replied Happy the red bird,
and they dashed off through
the snowy white woods.

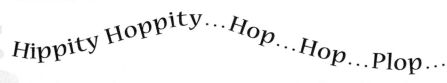

Hippity Hoppity…Hop…Hop…Plop…

But suddenly, Happy the red bird stopped.
"Listen," he whispered, "Do you hear
what I hear? Someone is crying."

In the distance sparkled a little snowman
in a tattered scarf and hat with
four beautiful heart ♡ shaped buttons
all the way down his front.
Bun-Bun and Happy quietly drew near.

Bun-Bun asked the snowman,
"Why do you cry?"

"I'm lonely," he replied with a sniff.
"The children who made me into
a snowman stopped coming to play."

"Then come with us," invited Bun-Bun.
"We're on an adventure to
follow the light. We'll be back before day.

 Hippity…  Hop…Flippity Flap

into the night...Following the Light...

Friends make the journey more fun!

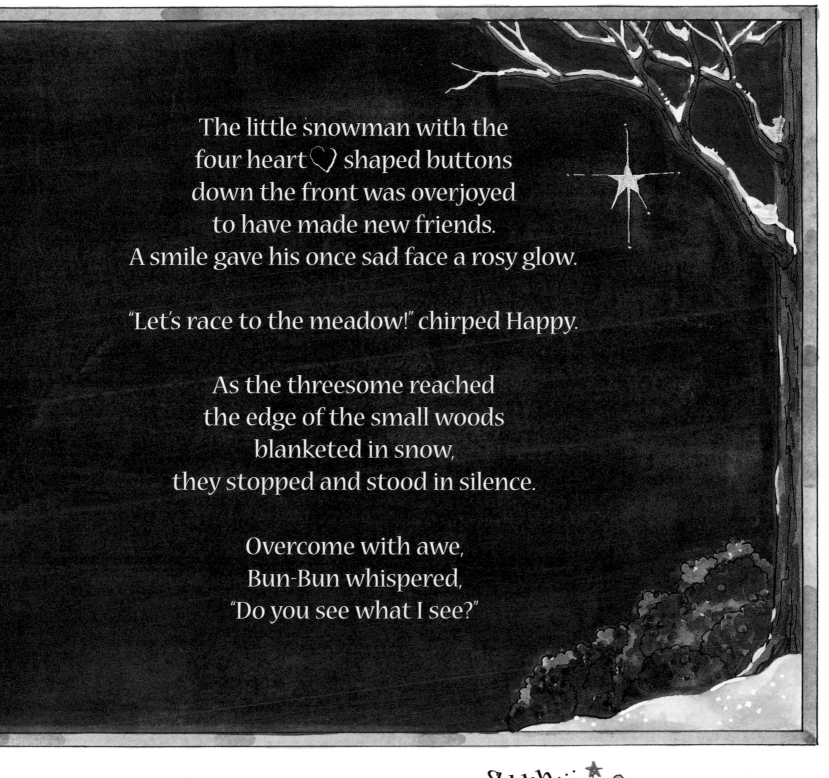

The little snowman with the
four heart ♡ shaped buttons
down the front was overjoyed
to have made new friends.
A smile gave his once sad face a rosy glow.

"Let's race to the meadow!" chirped Happy.

As the threesome reached
the edge of the small woods
blanketed in snow,
they stopped and stood in silence.

Overcome with awe,
Bun-Bun whispered,
"Do you see what I see?"

Shhhh...

The dancing light was from a star…
a star so bright, that it beckoned,
"Come follow me!"

Bun-Bun wanted so badly
to follow this miraculous star,
but remembered her mother,
father, and brothers
still snuggled in their nest.
They would be worried
if she ventured too far.

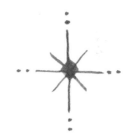

The star silently floated further
into the far reaches of the night.

"We'll follow the star,"
Bun-Bun told her friends.
"But we must be home
before morning light."

Wheeeeee! Wheeeeeeeeee! Wheeeeeeeeeeeeee...!

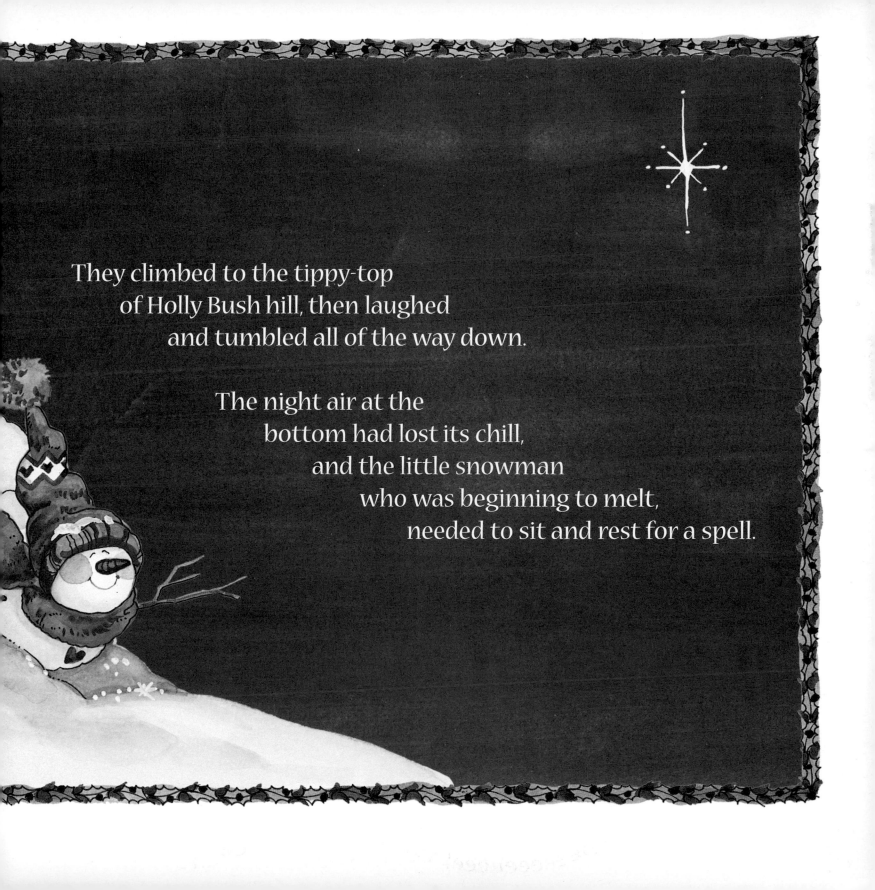

They climbed to the tippy-top
   of Holly Bush hill, then laughed
     and tumbled all of the way down.

      The night air at the
        bottom had lost its chill,
          and the little snowman
            who was beginning to melt,
              needed to sit and rest for a spell.

The group stopped to rest for a bit.
Bun-Bun and the snowman
began to clap and sing,
while Happy danced about.

Over the river and through the woods to grandma's house we go...

From the shadows,
a soft voice began to join in.
"Baa…Baa…Baa…
Maaay I join in your gathering?"

It was Baa-Baa, the lamb.
Her shepherds had also
been following the star,
but she was chasing a
firefly and had
wandered too far.

So the foursome set off again
and soon topped the next hill.
Below was a city.
Suddenly the wondrous star stood still,
shining directly on a little stable:
It was a beautiful sight to behold.

All of the animals—
and even the little snowman
with the four heart
shaped buttons—agreed
that this must be a special
place and a special
night, indeed.

But as they tumbled down the hill, Bun-Bun worried. The valley was quite warm, and her new-found friend made of snow was melting even more. "You musn't go on," Bun-Bun warned.

But the little snowman who was now quite thin said, "I must go on! I want to see why the star has stopped right over the stable."

Happy, the red bird had flown ahead
and peeked inside the stable's window.

"Don't give up, now!" he urged.
"You must see what I've seen!"
And at that moment,
Happy the red bird without a song
burst into the sweetest of lullabies.
Bun-Bun, Baa-Baa, and the little snowman
listened in amazement.
They hurried inside to see for
themselves what had given
Happy such a sweet song to sing.

In the manger, wrapped in a blanket and resting on the st

v—a heavenly sight—was a newborn baby, bathed in light.

As Happy the red bird sang his new song,
Bun-Bun and Baa-Baa felt compelled
to bow before the babe asleep in the straw.
They turned to the little snowman…
but he was gone.

All they could see was a hat, tattered
scarf and the four sparkling red heart  shaped
buttons glistening like never before.

Bun-Bun gently picked up one of the hearts
and placed it in the manger. The little
snowman's heart would never be lonely
again, and this was a comfort to her.

The animals knew that they must go,
if they were to be home before dawn.
Baa-Baa gave Bun-Bun a farewell
hug as she left to rejoin her flock
down in the meadow.

"Baaa...Baaa...Baaa...," she called, "Maaa...Maaa..., is that you?"

The twosome hurried home. Just as
the first rays of morning light began to
appear, Bun-Bun snuggled into the nest
where the family was still sleeping.
She pondered the star of wonder and the
beautiful baby asleep in the hay.
She thought of the lonely little snowman
who wasn't lonely anymore, and the lamb
who had lost her way but found it again.
Then she fell sound asleep.

Now I lay me down to sleep...

Now each time it snows in these small woods,
Bun-Bun and the other animals
gather to build a snow friend
with a hat and a tattered scarf.

Remembering the beautiful heart ♥ she gave to the baby,
Bun-Bun carefully places three red heart ♥ shaped
buttons all the way down the snow friend's front
and joins with Happy the red bird
in singing a sweet song of joy in
celebration of the wonders of Christmas.

♫ "Rejoice…Rejoice…and again we say Rejoice!" ♫